For Better or For Worse:®
Grandpas Are for Jumping On

Lynn Johnston

TOR®

A TOM DOHERTY ASSOCIATES BOOK
NEW YORK

A Tor Book
Published by Tom Doherty Associates, Inc.
49 West 24th Street
New York, N.Y. 10010

ISBN: 0-812-50986-2

First Tor edition: September 1990

Printed in the United States of America

0 9 8 7 6 5 4 3 2 1

FOR EASTER IS NOT A TIME
FOR SADNESS, BUT A
TIME FOR REJOICING.
JUST AS SPRING AWAKENS
SLEEPING FLOWERS
AND ANIMALS AFTER A
LONG, COLD WINTER,
SO EASTER AWAKENS
US TO THE WONDERS
AND THE LOVE ALL
AROUND....

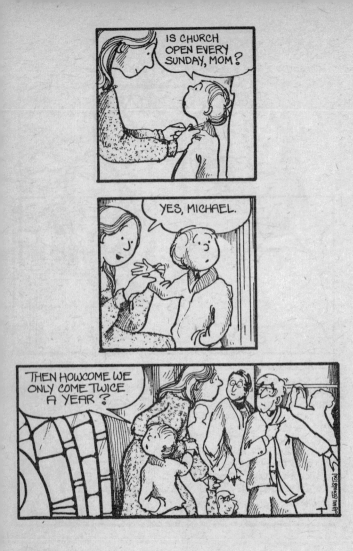

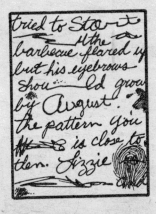

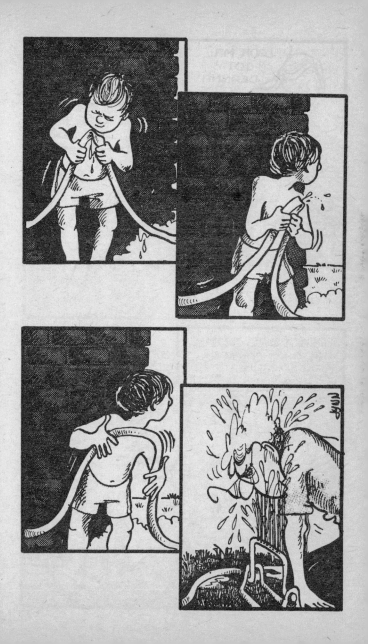

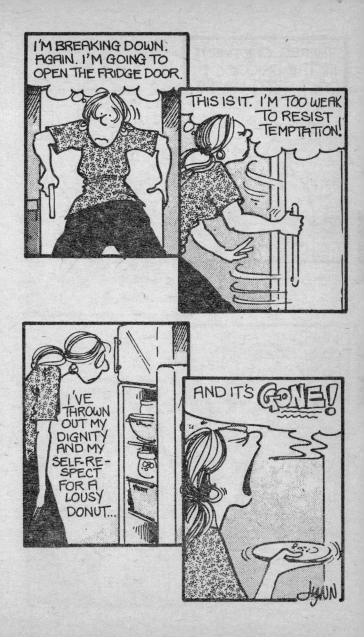